Heartprints

P. K. Hallinan

ideals children's books.
Nashville, Tennessee

First printing this edition 2002

ISBN-13: 978-0-8249-5450-5
ISBN-10: 0-8249-5450-5

Published by Ideals Children's Books
An imprint of Ideals Publications
A Guideposts Company
Nashville, Tennessee
www.idealsbooks.com

Printed and bound in Mexico by RR Donnelley

Cover Design by Jenny Hancock

Library of Congress Cataloging-in-Publication Data
Hallinan, P. K.
      Heartprints / written and illustrated by P. K. Hallinan.
        p. cm.
      Summary: Illustration and rhyming text show how we can brighten
the world with acts of kindness and caring.
      [1. Conduct of life—Fiction. 2. Stories in rhyme.] I. Title.
      PZ8.3.H15He   1999
  [E]-dc21   98-31281
                             CIP
                             AC

RRD-Rey_Feb14_8

For Jeanne, whose heartprints are strewn like flowers everywhere she goes.

How many heartprints
Will you leave today?
Will you share with a friend . . .

Will you give hugs away?

Will you listen with patience
To what others say?
How many heartprints
Will you leave today?

A heartprint is formed
When you do something kind.
Your love touches others,
Leaving heartprints behind.

So . . . what will you do?
Well, that's up to you.

You can smile at people
You pass on the street.

You can offer a handshake
To someone you meet.

You can even pitch in
For an hour or two
To help out a friend
With too much to do.

Yes, each little kindness
Leaves heartprints that say,
"A very nice person
Has been here today!"

Sometimes you'll reach out
To someone in strife
And do something thoughtful
That changes a life.

Or sometimes you may say
The quietest thing
And never quite know
How you've made a heart sing.

But this much is certain,
Our heartprints hold fast
When others come first,
And we put ourselves last.

So . . . how many heartprints
Will you leave today?
Will you cheer up a teammate
Who's made the wrong play?

Will you share a few laughs
So a classmate will smile . . .

Or tend to a friend
Who's been ill for awhile?

Even a wink of your eye
Helps to show
You care about others
And you want them to know.

Yes, heartprints can heal us
With the power of love.
They lift up our spirits
Like the wings of a dove.

And it's joyful to know
In all that we do,
The heartprints we give out
Make *us* happy too!

So, offer your friendship
To each girl and boy,

And join in the music,
The singing, the joy,

And you'll brighten the world
As you go on your way.

How many heartprints
Will you leave today?